EVELYN'S TALES

By Evelyn Marsh

Illustrations by

Georgianna Chernowsky

Granddaughter of Author Evelyn Marsh

And

Kimberlee Andrulat

To order additional copies of this book, contact:
Xlibris Corporation
1-888-795-4274
www.Xlibris.com
Orders@Xlibris.com

This book was published as a tribute to Evelyn Fuegen Marsh who was a talented artist and story teller. She was inspired to write stories about events in her six children's lives. Her oldest boy's first eyeglasses (ELMERS EYEGLASSES) and her youngest boy's first eyeglasses (SPEC SPIDER) and another first airplane (PETER PLANE) etc.

Evelyn is greatly missed by her husband George and her six children.

HOWIE HIGHCHAIR

Little Howie Highchair was a sad-looking chair. He had been used for years and years and now Timmy didn't want to sit in him anymore.

"He's falling apart," Timmy said.

Poor little Howie shuddered a brittle little shiver through his stiff, broken frame.

"I'm sure to go out with the trash. Nobody can do anything for me now," thought Howie.

Father put Howie in the basement. The door closed and little Howie stood alone in a dark, dusty corner.

He heard mice come creeping out of their hiding places to peer at him. They poked and pushed with their wet pink noses. They even nibbled on his three good legs and one broken one. One little mouse climbed up on his seat and danced a jig, squeaking merrily all the while.

"A few weeks' of this and I shall be chewed up into a pile of sawdust," Howie worried.

The days came and went and Howie still stood in his corner listening to the mice playing, the furnace booming, and the water running through the pipes of the big house.

One day footsteps sounded by the basement door. The door opened and the light shone down the stairs. Father came down and turned on the light. Timmy trailed behind.

"There he is!" cried Timmy, running up to hug Howie, "Please, Daddy, I don't want him down here in the basement alone. Can you fix him?"

Father stood there looking and stroking his chin. He paused to think. "Well, Tim, I suppose we could do something about him, but he won't be a highchair anymore,"

"1 don't care what he'll be, as long as he lives upstairs with me again," said Timmy, hopping up and down on one foot.

Father got out his tools and started to work, smoothing and evening, tightening and shoring up. Timmy watched.

Before long, Howie's legs were all the same size, making him look sleek and ready for anything.

"Well, that feels better now," thought Howie, "I wonder what's next?"

He soon found out.

Father glued Howie's arms on tight and fixed his back up with a large, smooth piece of wood. Then he put a new seat on Howie.

"My, my," mused Howie, "I certainly don't feel like my old self anymore!"

Timmy looked on in wonder. "He looks beautiful, Daddy!"

Father went to the shelf and got down some paints. "We'll be finished after this last step," said Father.

He painted Howie's arms and legs bright blue with shiny red stripes.

"Look at him now!" squealed Timmy.

"He needs one more thing," Father said, and started to paint again. "And then he'll officially be the new and improved Howie."

When Father stood up, Timmy saw how special Howie really had become. "Daddy, he looks just like me now! He has big blue eyes and a great big smile. You even painted on some yellow hair."

Father smiled and ruffled Timmy's hair.

Howie's paint was soon dry.

"Let's take him back upstairs now, Timmy," said Father.

Father carried Howie up the stairs, down the hall, and into the living room.

"The best chair in the house for Timmy," said Father with a smile.

"I am part of the family again," thought Howie, very happy indeed. He wore his big new smile with pride.

ELMER'S EYEGLASSES

Elmer was a big gray elephant who lived in the jungle. Now almost everyone knows that elephants cannot see very well. But Elmer could hardly see at all. He wouldn't even know you were there unless he was standing on top of you.

Poor Elmer had a real problem. He had to hold another elephant's tail so that he could follow the great herd. When the animals saw him coming, they got out of his way; he might step on them by mistake.

One day, the elephants took Elmer to the wise old owl who lived high up in a tree in the jungle.

"Please help us, Mr. Owl. Elmer is always stumbling and bumping into things. He can hardly see at all. What can we do to help him!"

Mr. Owl sat for a while, blinking his all-knowing eyes. Then he told them that Elmer needed glasses.

"Glasses!" trumpeted the herd. "Where can Elmer get glasses!"

"Elmer can get glasses in the big city," said Mr. Owl.

The elephants thanked Mr. Owl and led Elmer to the edge of the jungle. "Stay on this road, Elmer, and you will come to the big city," said the elephants. "Good-bye, good-bye, good luck, 'Elmer!" called his elephant friends.

Elmer walked on and on, He knew he was coming to the city because he heard car horns blowing at him as they went by.

"How will I know when I get to an eyeglass store?" wondered Elmer. "I will have to ask questions."

Into town he bumbled. Elmer knew he was near a fruit store. He could smell it. He was so near, he was standing knee-deep in bananas. The fruit man was yelling so loudly that Elmer could not ask him where the eyeglass store was. Poor Elmer stumbled away.

Then he thought he saw an animal blinking at him in the middle of the road. Elmer thumped over to the strange sight and squashed the traffic light flat. How could Elmer know it was a light and not an animal? He could hardly see.

Big, wet tears rolled down his trunk. *Plop, plop, plop.* They fell onto the road. "I'll never find an eyeglass store!" he wailed.

A little boy saw Elmer crying in the road. "Why are you crying?" he asked.

"Who are you?" asked Elmer. I cannot see you very well."

"I am Billy. Now tell me why you're crying," the boy said.

"My name is Elmer and I am looking for an eyeglass store. The owl said I need glasses,"

"I can show you," said Billy. "I will ride on your trunk so that you don't step on me."

"Climb on, Billy, and show me the way."

Down the street the two of them went, with Billy telling Elmer which way to go. Soon they were at a store that sold eyeglasses in every shape, color, and size, for men and women and girls and boys.

The optician was very frightened when Elmer came in.

"Get out! Get out! I'll call the police!" he shouted.

"No," said Billy. Elmer only wants a pair of eyeglasses to see better. He won't hurt you."

"Are you sure he will not step on me?" asked the optician as he watched Elmer squash a chair he tried to sit on.

"I'm sure," Billy said.

"But I don't know where I can get glasses big enough to fit Elmer," he said. "Let me think for a minute."

The optician rubbed his chin for a while, and then disappeared into the back of the store. When he came out, he had a screw driver and a tall ladder. "Don't go away," he said to Billy and Elmer. "And please, don't walk around in my store," he said to Elmer. "I'll be right back."

Elmer and Billy waited. They heard scraping noises outside, but they stayed put, just like the man told them.

The eyeglass man finally came back in, carrying a big pair of eyeglasses. They were the biggest ones Billy ever saw. The optician proudly put them on Elmer. They were a perfect fit.

"I can see, I can see, I can see very well!" trumpeted Elmer. "I am so happy!"

"Where did you get those glasses?" asked Billy.

The optician laughed. "Right outside," he said, "hanging over my door."

Elmer and Billy looked puzzled.

The man explained. "They were part of my store's sign!"

Elmer and Billy and the eyeglass man laughed together.

"Thank you," said Elmer. "Now I will go back to my home in the jungle."

When Elmer reached his jungle home, all his friends came to meet him. "Those are the nicest glasses we ever saw," they all said.

Elmer was so happy. He could see his friends and all of the jungle now. He also felt very special, because he was the only one in the jungle who ever went to town to get a pair of eyeglasses.

SANTA'S GREEN ELF

A little green elf stood sadly by,

Holding back tears and wondering why,

"Everything I do, I do wrong.

This can't go on for very long.

The toys that I make soon fall apart.

Woe is me; it saddens my heart.

Why don't toys stay together for me?

I do my job so miserably.

Oh, I shall be sent away from here,

Far from Santa, who I love so dear!"

Just then Santa came through the door.

The green elf's heart sank to the floor.

But Santa was smiling a small smile,

And stroking his beard all the while.

"I've been thinking of a job for you,

A job I'm sure, I know, you'll do.

You'll take apart old broken-down toys

Sent to us by girls and boys.

I need the wheels, springs, nuts, bolts and screws

Because these parts we have to use.

These are to be used on next year's toys

For Christmas, for all girls and boys.

Some elves are meant to take things apart.

Now, my green elf, why don't you start?"

The little green elf grabbed the old toys

And started to work with great noise.

He put the parts away in a box,

A big red box with silver locks.

"I've done my job," he smiled to himself.

"Truly I am Santa's green elf."

PETER PLANE

There once was a little wood plane named Peter. He belonged to a little boy named Tommy. Tommy flew Peter every day by the big airport and, as each day passed, Peter grew sadder and sadder.

"I want to fly where the big silver planes go," thought Peter.

Just then a mighty gust of wind took Peter higher and higher. Up, up, up where the big silver planes fly. A shiver of delight ran through his little wood frame.

"I can see everything from up here!" cried Peter.

He flew on and on and on. Peter flew over the town and the green fields. Up, up, up high over the mountains he soared.

"How big the world is!" said Peter.

Dipping and swooping, Peter had such fun until he looked down for Tommy and could not see him. Big tears started to run down his nose. It was then he heard a deep voice.

"Who is that?" asked Peter.

"It is I, the North Wind! What are you doing up here all alone! Why are you crying!" he roared.

"I only wanted to see the world the way the big planes do, but I am lost and I miss Tommy," sniffed Peter. "It isn't any fun to see the world alone."

"Dip your wings and turn around," said the North Wind. "I shall blow you back to your friend. I hope you learned your lesson. Now you know that a little wood plane should not fly where big silver planes go."

Whoosh, whoosh, whoosh, the North Wind blew Peter back over the mountain to the green fields, until Peter saw the town where Tommy lived.

Peter dived down, down, down, straight into Tommy's back yard.

Tommy saw him coming and was happy that Peter had come back home.

Peter never flew away from Tommy again.

CHARLIE CATERPILLAR

A little soft caterpillar crept softly over the leaves. He had long brown fur with orange stripes. His friends called him Charlie.

Charlie was a very unhappy caterpillar. He wanted to go where all his friends could go. But all he could do was creep along. His mother said that someday he would be able to do what all his friends did, but Charlie was still said.

He saw a bird. "When can I fly like you, my friend?" he asked.

"Soon, soon, soon," chirped the bird.

Charlie then saw a bee. "When can I smell the flowers like you, my friend?"

"Soon, soon, soon," buzzed the bee.

Charlie crawled along until he met a shiny black cricket. "Can you tell me when I can hop from grass to grass?" Charlie asked.

"Soon, soon, soon," creaked the cricket.

All summer long, Charlie crept along. Then one day he felt the wind growing colder. "I must find a warm place to stay, because winter is coming," he said.

Charlie crept up onto a tree branch and started to build a warm white house around himself. He was so-o-o sleepy.

The winter wind blew his branch and the snow fell softly on his house, but Charlie slept on. Then one day spring came and melted the snow and Charlie woke up. "1 will have to leave my safe house," he thought.

He nibbled his way through his warm nest. "How bright the light is. 1 feel so strange," said Charlie. He lay on the branch for a long time. When he finally moved, he found that he had a pair of bright butterfly wings. "How pretty they are!" he thought.

Charlie swooped off the branch to the grass below. Charlie hopped from grass to grass. He flew from flower to flower, smelling each one as he went along. Charlie went up, up, up, and swooped and flew just like a bird. "I am so happy," he said.

When the birds, bees and crickets saw Charlie, they were happy too.

"Everyone was right," said Charlie. "They told me I would do what they could do, soon, soon, soon ."

MR. ELMER NOBODY SOMEBODY

Night crept softly around the house, closing it in tight. The rain had been falling all day, and now it was finally stopping.

"Oh, fine," said Tommy with the big feet. "It stops now, when we can't go out to play."

"Rain stop, rain stop," squealed little Susie who repeats everything she hears.

Linda just sat there with her long brown braids hanging in front of her face, saying nothing but feeling mad, mad, mad. She was so mad she could cry.

They were all shiny clean from their baths and were waiting for Mother to finish making supper.

Father called them over to him and they all snuggled down on the large red sofa in front of the hissing, crackling fireplace. Long shadows danced on the walls and floor while good smells came from the kitchen.

"Children," Father began, "you should have a friend to play with on rainy days like today. I used to have a friend just for bad days when I was a little boy."

"You did?" they asked, their eyes alive with excitement. "Who was he? What did he look like? What did you play?"

"I can't tell you what he looked like, but I can tell you his name. Mr. Elmer Nobody Somebody. And we played make believe. He was the captain of my ship and the pilot of my airplane sometimes, and sometimes we just sat and talked together," said Father. "Now that I'm talking about him, I think he is in the room right now."

Three pairs of eyes stole peeks at all the shadowy corners and doors.

"Where is he is now?" asked Tommy.

"I think he's by the woodpile near the fireplace," said Linda.

"I see, I see," said Susie, wriggling around.

"Why don't you look for Elmer before supper and have a chat with him? That is, if you can find him," laughed Father.

Tommy dove headfirst into the closet. All you could see were two big feet sticking out.

Linda poked around in the woodpile and looked under the chairs.

Little Susie jumped up and down on the sofa, yelling, "I see Emer! I see Emer!"

"Where! Where!" yelled Tommy and Linda as they came running back to the sofa. "Where is he, Susie?"

"Everywhere!" giggled Susie.

Father laughed. "Susie was the first to find him, because she made believe. Linda and Tommy, you couldn't see him right away because you had almost forgotten to make believe for fun."

Everybody was laughing when Mother called them in for dinner.

The table was set for five people.

"Mother, you forgot a plate," said Tommy.

"Yes," said Linda. "We have company for supper tonight."

"Goodness gracious, who?" asked Mother.

"Emer, Emer," sang Susie, dancing around the table.

"Elmer," said Father, winking at Mother.

"Elmer?" said Mother, thinking a moment.

"Oh yes, we can't forget him, can we? I haven't thought of him for years," laughed Mother.

And she ran off to the kitchen to get another plate for Mr. Elmer Nobody Somebody.

THE TAIL OF MIKE MONKEY

Once upon a time, in the great green jungle, there lived a little brown monkey named Mike. Though he lived with a large family of monkeys, he was very lonely.

All the other monkeys laughed and made fun of him because poor Mike had no tail at all. They would swing by their tails all around him as he sat on his lonely little tree branch.

Poor little Mike couldn't stand it any longer, so one day he very quietly climbed down his lonely tree and left his home.

As he was walking along a jungle trail, he heard a loud banging noise. A lion went rushing by Mike without giving him a second look. Other wild animals went running by, too.

Mike quickly climbed up the nearest tree to see what was making all the loud noises and what was chasing the animals.

From his lofty perch, high in the tree, Mike saw strange-looking animals walking on two feet and banging on large cans.

"I wonder why they are doing that!" Mike said to himself.

Just then, a loud roar rang through the jungle. Mike saw a lion trapped in a large net. The strange-looking animals put him in a big cage and he could not get out.

Mike was one scared little monkey.

"I must warn the other monkeys! Even though they made fun of me, I am still one of them."

He quickly climbed down the tree and ran as fast as he could down the jungle trail.

When Mike got back home, all the monkeys laughed at him as he told them his story.

"Look at Mike, he has no tail, so now he is trying to make one up," they howled.

With that, a loud banging noise was heard. All the monkeys went rushing about their homes in the trees, even little Mike.

The strange-looking animals that walked on two feet started to climb the trees and soon caught all the monkeys by their tails, but they could not catch lucky Mike, because he had no tail.

"Woe is us," cried the monkeys as they were being put in a big cage.

Mike watched from a safe tree as the two-legged animals made camp.

When all was quiet in the camp, Mike crept softly down the tree and let all the monkeys free. They ran far, far away.

From that time on, Mike was no longer lonely. The monkeys never laughed at him again. Mike was their hero.

THE BUNNY'S BUMBLE

There was once a very unhappy bunny. He thought his ears were too long and his tail was too short and fluffy. While he was sitting and complaining, a great wind came by and blew his tail and ears away.

The poor bunny chased after them, but he couldn't catch them.

How all the animals laughed when they saw the bunny!

The unhappy bunny went to ask Mr. Owl what he could do to get his tail and ears back.

"You must go around the world and meet the great wind on its way back. Your ears and tail might blow back on again," said the wise old owl.

The bunny put on a topcoat, sunglasses, and a top hat and sailed out onto the ocean on a big ship. He was going to meet the great wind.

When the ship docked in Africa, he hopped down the gangplank.

In the marketplace he saw a snake charmer, a pottery maker, stands of fruits and spices and many other things. He soon found a camel train leaving for the desert where the great wind blows.

Even with the hot sun glaring down, Bunny would not take off his clothes. He was so ashamed of the way he looked. When the camel train reached the oasis, he lay down by a pool of water.

Suddenly he saw the great wind coming across the desert, kicking up the sand. He ran to meet it.

The bunny took off his coat, hat, and sunglasses when the wind blew over him.

It soon passed and the bunny heard the camels' snickering behind him. Over he hopped to the pool, wondering why they were laughing.

He looked at himself in the water. Bunny saw the strangest-looking rabbit peering back at him.

"Woe is me. I should never have complained about the way I looked before. Look at me now!"

The bunny now wore a lion's tail and bushy mane.

"I wish that I had been happy with my own ears and tail. Now I know that you should be happy with what you've got, for you may end up looking like you are not."

CLEM CLAM

Clem was just a baby clam. He lived with his family in a clam bed where the water was cool, dark, and deep.

Clem was tired of laying in one place day after day. His mother always warned him about the creature with five arms. She told him, "Little clams are safer in their clam beds!"

Little Clem would not listen, so one day Clem said, "I will go out and see the rest of the ocean floor. Nothing can harm me." Then Clem hopped out of his clam bed and skittered along the sand.

The green and brown seaweed waved at Clem as he skittered by. It seemed to wave him on. "It cannot harm me," said Clem. "I am safe."

Clem saw little fishes playing games on the ocean floor. When they saw Clem they asked, "Clem, why aren't you in your clam bed?"

Clem replied, "I'm off to see the rest of the ocean floor. Nothing can harm me."

The little fishes warned Clem as they swam away. "You will be sorry!"

A curious brown spotted seahorse came up to Clem, but it soon swam away. "Nothing can harm me. I am safe," said Clem.

Suddenly he saw a beautiful red starfish. Clem skittered over to it. The starfish reached out his five arms to catch Clem. Clem was so scared! He remembered what his mother had said about the creature with five arms. He bumped and skittered his way back home.

"Mother was right. I am safer in my little clam bed," said a much wiser Clem.

SPEC SPIDER

Once upon a time there lived a family of spiders in a cool, dark cellar.

Now Mother Spider had many, many children. She named every little spider but one. "Oh, dear, I can't think of one single name to give him," said Mother Spider.

As time passed, the little spiders grew bigger and bigger.

One day Mother Spider gathered all her children around her and said, "Children, it is time for you to go to spinning school."

Off they trooped, two by two, even the little spider without a name. Mother marched them into the spinning school and said, "Here you will learn to spin a home, as all spiders must do."

The days passed, and the first report cards were sent home. Mother Spider looked at all of them. She was very pleased with her little spiders' marks, except for the card that had no name.

"It says here that every time you try to spin a web, it has so many holes in it that even a big horsefly could fly right through it," said Mother Spider. "What is the matter with you, little spider with no name!"

Just then, they all heard a soft knock on their door. It was the school doctor. He said, "Mother Spider, I stopped by to tell you that little Spider had all his eyes examined yesterday and he needs glasses."

"No wonder he can't spin a web without holes!" Mother Spider replied.

The very next day, she took her little spider by his hands and went to the eye doctor for glasses. When Mother Spider saw little spider with his new glasses on, she exclaimed, "Oh, little spider, I finally have a name for you! I shall call you 'Spec.' And it goes very well with 'spider,' if I do say so myself."

From that day on, the little spider without a name was called "Spec Spider," and a better spinner of webs couldn't be found anywhere.